EXPRESS NEWSPAPERS plc, Ludgate House,
245 Blackfriars Road,
London SE1 9UX.

Produced by Brainwaves Limited
5 Highwood Ridge, Hatch Warren, Basingstoke,
Hampshire RG22 4UU.

ISBN 0–85079–251–7

Printed and bound in Singapore.

RUPERT

and the Time Machine

One sunny day, Rupert, Edward and Algy decide to visit their friend the Wise Old Goat at his castle. 'Hello!' he says as they arrive. 'Do come in and have a glass of lemonade!' While the pals wait for him to return, Rupert shows Edward the History Clock. 'What is it?' asks Edward. 'It's a time machine,' replies Rupert. 'It can send you spinning backwards into the past!'

As Rupert is talking to Edward, Algy peers at the control panel. 'Ooh!' he says to himself, 'How interesting . . . I wonder what happens if I pull this lever?'

Suddenly the History Clock begins to hum, and Rupert and Edward start to disappear. 'Oh no!' cries Algy. 'I must have sent them back in time!' 'You should know better than to meddle with strange machines!' says the Wise Old Goat when he comes back and learns what has happened.

'They're not wearing Return Medals, and without them they can't get back!' 'What can we do? Where are they?' wails Algy. 'They're in the time of the dinosaurs,' says the Wise Old Goat, 'millions of years ago. You must go back with the Return Medals and find them!'

'Ooh, I'm dizzy! Where's Nutwood gone?' groans Edward, as the two friends suddenly find themselves in a strange, rocky landscape, next to a pile of huge eggs.

'One's hatching out!' cries Rupert. 'Look, it's a baby brontosaurus!' The next moment there's a terrifying screech as a group of pterodactyls swoop down towards the pals. 'Quick, pick up the baby!' shouts Edward. 'We must find somewhere to hide!' 'I think I can see a cave over there,' says Rupert. 'If we hurry we might just reach it in time . . .'

The chums are trapped in the cave. 'We can't go out there,' gulps Rupert, 'it's far too dangerous!' Then he spots a glimmer of light at the back of the cave. 'Let's go and see what's there,' he suggests to Edward.

'Oooh!' the pals gasp as they come out into a glittering cavern. 'Fireflies!' Edward shouts gleefully. Then Rupert notices another tunnel behind him. 'I think we should try up here!' he says, and they start to crawl upwards.

The pals climb out into the daylight and are amazed to see a giant brontosaurus glaring at them. But to Rupert's surprise the huge creature seems quite friendly, bending her long neck down towards the pals. 'I'm sure she's the baby's mother!' cries Rupert. Then the baby brontosaurus gives a yelp of delight and clambers on to its mother's back.

'Let's climb up too!' calls Rupert. As they do so, the pals suddenly hear a loud roar, together with what sounds exactly like someone calling 'Help!'

'Look!' cries Rupert. 'There's Algy – he must've been sent here by the Wise Old Goat to help us get back!' 'But he's being attacked by a huge Tyrannosaurus Rex!' exclaims Edward. 'He'll be in *real* trouble if we don't do something very quickly!'

Sure enough, on the far side of a clearing the two pals can see poor Algy trapped up a tree, yelling for help. 'Don't worry, we're coming!' shouts Rupert. 'Just hang on tight! We won't be long!' calls Edward, encouragingly.

The mother brontosaurus hears Rupert calling to Algy and turns to look at him. 'My friend is in terrible danger!' he explains. 'We must try and save him from that huge Tyrannosaurus Rex!'

'Do you think she'll help us?' asks Edward. 'I hope so,' says Rupert, 'she seems to understand . . .'

The next thing the two pals know, the giant creature begins to thunder at high speed across the clearing, the ground shaking as she charges. As she gets nearer the tree where Algy is stranded, Rupert and Edward start waving their arms and shouting 'Shoo!' With one last look at Algy's legs, the Tyrannosaurus hesitates, then slinks off towards another clump of trees. 'Hurrah!' cheers Rupert. 'We did it!'

old friends!' cries Rupert. Pressing the buttons on their medals, the pals go straight back to the Wise Old Goat's castle. 'What a relief!' he cries, as they reappear in the History Clock, safe and sound.

'Phew! That was a narrow escape!' sighs Algy, as the brontosaurus lets him climb on her back. Algy quickly hands over a Return Medal to both his chums, and the three of them slide off the creature's neck. 'Goodbye,